HIJACKED HOLIDAYS

B. A. PAUL

CONTENTS

FOREWORD

Not everyone has fond memories of the holidays. Be it a family crisis or the lack of a family, burnt turkey or the lack of a turkey, sometimes our perfectly planned Norman Rockwell imaginings come out lopsided.

These tales reflect the frustration of those not-so-pristine holidays. Something's a tiny bit skewed—or totally amiss.

Whether you need a short escape from Aunt Bertha's blathering or a companion to hide away with while Uncle Rodger hooks up his RV in your backyard, Hijacked Holidays has you covered.

Happy reading!

B. A. Paul

GOOD HELP

Finding someone to take over long-established holiday traditions can be a tricky business.

Faye dunked the last mixing bowl caked in brownie batter into the sink. The suds disappeared five dirty bowls and two spatulas ago and her preferred burn-the-hide-off water temperature for handwashing dishes was now only lukewarm. She'd done as much prep as possible for today—the last round of family would trickle in for the third and final holiday dinner of the season.

She gazed out the window to her backyard as she absent-mindedly swished the dishrag into the bowl. A towering oak taller than the house supported a rickety tree swing rope—minus the wooden seat. The frayed end danced in the breeze. She'd wanted her son to replace the seat before the holidays. Give the little ones a place to cut loose and feel the wind on their faces—instead of feeling the wrath of Faye inside for being too rambunctious around her vintage snowman collection.

Her son was too busy, as were the sons-in-law.

As were the grandsons-in-law and various fiancés capable of ladder-climbing and tree-swing seat replacing.

She and Albert had created quite the brood. You'd think one of her guys could handle such a menial task. Faye never asked for much, but when she did, no one was available.

What was that old nursery rhyme? Miss Muffet? The Old Maid?

No. It was a chicken. The Red Hen or something like that.

Good help was just so hard to come by. Faye felt like a molting red chicken. Carrying the load of family rearing alone as Albert galivanted across the country under the guise of providing for their family—which he did, for the most part—but it was Faye who made each penny stretch triple-time while Albert "stretched" his love out from coast to coast. Also triple-time, come to find out.

When confronted, Albert had blamed his hot-trotting on being a red-headed stepchild with no good father figure. Nevertheless, he fathered a few red-headed children of his own, also with no real father figure around.

Albert and Faye Crawley and their five children were dubbed the Crawley Crew by neighbors and social circles decades ago. All five of her kids natural redheads. All five grown, married, and relatively successful with multiple offspring of their own—not all redheads, thank goodness. And some of those children were bound and determined to make her Great Grandma Faye by the end of the upcoming year. With so many adults and jobs and travel in the mix, the three big holiday meals were a necessity.

And she hosted and baked and cooked for each one, politely asking for help and being refused over and over.

No one could cook like her, they said.

They'd just be in the way, they said.

No one could clean up to her liking, they said.

She supposed they were right. She supposed her finickiness was the main reason most of her family dared not help her. But she knew her mind and she knew how things were to be. Especially in the realm of the kitchen.

And more so in the realm of family affairs. Faye's eldest grandson duly nick-named her Hawkeye. For if it happened in the Crawley family, Faye saw it. Sometimes before "it" even happened. A bad relationship. A bad financial decision. A bad turn of a teenager toward the dark side…

If it weren't for her and her hawk eyes, half of her brood would have wandered away to flail helplessly in the wind. Or been in jail.

Or worse.

Faye straightened her back. Pride surging through her spine. No. No one cared as much as Faye did, which gave her excellent eyesight over all things Crawly Crew. Like which marriage would last—she called two of the divorces three years before they happened, and squawked and henpecked, running off no fewer than three grandchildren's fiancés. Or at least that's what everyone else thought.

That they ran away.

Everyone except perhaps Gloria. That dear grandchild was special, gifted from above and from Faye's influence with the all-seeing, all-feeling burden of watch care. Faye looked over her shoulder at Gloria who was standing in one of Faye's old aprons, chopping onions and tomatoes for the salad. Faye touched a hand to her own apron pocket, the carefully wrapped gift was still in place. The box was no bigger than a deck of cards, but Faye was looking forward to gifting this tiny package more than anything in the world…

Gloria was humming "Frosty the Snowman" as she went

along her work, her bright blonde ponytail bobbing to the tune.

Snowman.

Faye smiled as she turned back to her dishes. She couldn't have designed a more flawless helper as Gloria.

Over the years, Faye used her ever-more arthritic hands and elbows to buckle down and kept to the task of feeding the holiday gangs all on her own. With Gloria as her only sou chef and snowman duster. Perhaps these festivities kept her just spry enough to avoid depression in the dreary winters. They also gave her something to piddle with come Independence Day when the massive Crawley Crew rented out all of Lake Walnut's cabins and Faye would put on a summer spread like no one's business.

And her family would pitch in and gift her one more vintage paper mâché snowman for her efforts. Faye came to expect that yearly gift. So lovingly bestowed upon her by family who wanted nothing much to do with her the rest of the year, aside from drama mitigator and baker, that is.

Faye sighed and pulled the bowl from the sink, shaking off the excess water and placing it on the drying mat. Stainless steel and dinged and scratched. Albert bought her that mixing set the year before he—

She shook off the intrusive memory and tapped at the bottom of the bowl, as if tousling the hair of a beloved grandchild.

She knew she was getting too old to handle all three dinners—two of them nearly back-to-back. And she knew this would be her last year. She spoke with Gloria this past summer at the cabin. "Give me one more season. Then it's all yours. The recipe box. The mixing bowl set. The spatulas."

Gloria's eyes had widened. Clearly, this grandchild had never imagined Grandma Faye would choose her to carry on the traditions.

"And Gloria," Faye said. "The snowmen will be yours, too." The 25-year-old had turned all shades of white and had nearly fallen off the picnic bench. That summer's snowman sat between them.

About the size of a two-slice toaster tipped on its end, the snowman was likely purchased off eBay or some antique site. Faye had started her collection with just two—passed down from her own mother. Those originals were dingy and yellow with dust and time. The one on the picnic bench was a little brighter, but not by much. The black hat was coming off the snowman's head at the back (but that was perfectly fine). Its carrot nose was a bit turned up at the end. His adornment was a four-leaf clover, and he had a matching green scarf. Faye best loved the snowmen which represented holidays other than the typical winter ones.

Her favorite was a Valentine's Day themed one, complete with a rickety wooden bow-and-arrow and a fabric scarf dotted with little pink hearts.

Gloria had toyed with the edge of the hat. Peeking inside.

"There's nothing in there yet, dear. That'll be your job. Watch carefully this year. Wait patiently. You'll know what to place under the hat come January."

Gloria beamed. If the snowman had been of snow instead of paper pulp, her glow would've melted it through the cracks in the picnic table.

Faye smiled again. Gloria was coming to the last stanza of the song, something about "Don't you cry..." Which was fitting because the onion was starting to burn her eyes, and she brushed her shoulder to her cheek.

She unstopped the sink and as the murky water swirled and gurgled down the drain, she turned to peek into the oven as she dried her knobby hands on a too-damp dishtowel. Side by side, the brownies began their ever-so-slight rise in the pan as the sweet potatoes softened under the glow of the heating element. She'd only add mini marshmallows to half of the pan. She stood and stretched, rubbing her back and shaking her head. Melody's newest fiancé (third in an ever-growing line) refused to eat marshmallows on his sweet potatoes.

Faye feared that particular granddaughter was lining herself up for another universe of pain with that idiot. Brian. Brian, the idiot who can't eat marshmallows—or heaven forbid, scrape them off. Melody saw him as her knight in shining armor. When would that girl learn these fools she picks out don't wear shiny armor? Guys like Matt and Tyler and Brian. These fools own only suits of selfish lust.

Gloria had learned this lesson the hard way at the ripe old age of twenty-one. Faye hated to be the one to break her heart, but the girl had to learn a lesson. And her choice in Fynn had been the perfect canvas on which to paint that lesson...

Melody was forever the hard-head and would need more convincing. Many canvases, Faye feared.

"Grandma, those marshmallows are spreading over to Brian's side." Gloria had bent down to inspect the baking goodies alongside Faye.

Both women rose. Faye put her arm around Gloria.

"And what would you do about this conundrum if it were your year to tackle this family all on your own?"

Gloria tipped her head at Faye, thinking. Her blue eyes danced in the kitchen light and then darting toward Faye's massive collection of paper mâché snow people. Each one donning a black hat. Each hat had come loose, just a tiny bit, either on its own or with a little help from Faye. The Four-Leaf Clover snowman sat front-and-center on the grand shelving display.

"The hat's already loose. Wouldn't take much."

Faye smiled and wrapped her arm around Gloria's shoulders. "Time to set the table, dear." The ladies heard the front door burst open, voices filling the foyer around the corner. A cold draft wafted at their feet as they moved in sync to set the plates.

"Looks great!"

"Smells wonderful."

The accolades dripped from the mouths of the slightly grateful as the full-blooded Crawley adults and their children filled the rooms, flinging packages and coats everywhere. Faye left Gloria to the table and went about organizing the incoming flock of chaos. "Packages under the tree, right? Coats in the spare room, right?" How many years? Good help is scarce, even in the most menial of tasks.

Faye helped one of the teen grandsons arrange packages largest in the back, smallest in the front under the Christmas tree. She was careful not to let her tiny package slip from her apron. She'd hoped to be done with the apron and this particular gift before everyone arrived, but alas. Time got away.

Faye pretended to care as the boy went on and on about his upcoming basketball tournament. Faye tried not to care about the endeavors too much until the love affairs started. That's when she'd have to turn her hawk eyes on and stand sentinel over Crawley hearts. As her mother had, so had Faye. Watching. Waiting. Taking care of things as they ought to be taken care of...

"—don't like marshmallows. Thanks for trying, though." Brian. Complaining. Already. Even as Gloria called everyone to the table.

Faye stood from her position next to the tree and straightened crooked candy cane ornament when she spied her youngest grandbaby, a little blonde-haired girl of four eyeing the shelves of snowmen. Before Faye could get her hips to swing her legs in the right direction, the girl had pulled one off the shelf and was turning it around and around in her chubby hands. The top hat was wobbly, the glue from decades ago losing its strength. "Look, Mamaw. There's somethin' under there."

Faye reached the child and gently took the snowman from her hands. The Valentine's Day one. It's a wonder the child hadn't shattered the bow and arrow adornment. She glanced back toward the dining room. Where was her mother? Good help... there just isn't any.

"See?" The girl peeked under the hat again, nose to nose with the snowman's carrot, and then looked up in utter wonder for spying the tuft of soft, red hair tucked under the hat. "It's like Mommy's hair."

"Yes, sweet child." Faye smoothed the heart-dotted scarf. The red lock of hair was secured in a bunch with a tiny dab of blue sewing thread and was threatening to fall from under the hat. Faye tucked it back in. She hadn't seen that bit of hair since the night Albert passed. She placed the piece on the highest shelf and also moved a few other rotund men up higher.

"That snowman has a secret, and if we say anything to anyone about what's under his hat, he'll melt all away." Faye flung her hands up in the air with flare, and the little girl giggled. "So we won't say the secret, right? Mamaw wouldn't want to lose a snowman. Not at Christmas."

The little girl's eyes widened and she shook her head. "Can I know the secret someday?"

Faye marched the girl toward the dining room where the rest of the family—save Melody and Gloria—had already taken their seats and had begun eating. "You'll have to ask Cousin Gloria when you're older."

Faye ensured everyone had what they needed—except Brian. He continued complaining about the selection and his special needs diet. And why hadn't Melody relayed his needs to the cooks...

Faye left before she smacked him down right in front of

everyone. She almost envied Gloria. Faye was about to miss out a long-awaited snowman moment so Gloria could take the reins. Would Gloria choose the natural cause of death route or the "never heard from again" method? Faye knew what she would choose, but it was Gloria's time to shine.

She found the young women on the front porch. Melody crying into Gloria's shoulder. Brian had obviously started his ranting well before their holiday meal was ready. Melody gathered herself when she saw Faye standing in the doorway. "Sorry Grandma. I just—"

"It's fine, dear, dinner's getting cold. Go on in." Faye gently grasped Melody's wrist as she passed. "The pain won't last forever, dear. All will be well soon." Melody smiled at her and went on. Faye reached for a shawl hanging by the door and stepped onto the porch with Gloria, the voices of family, the clinking of forks on plates and the smells of their hard work shut behind them for a moment.

"I think Brian's the one. The one for the four-leaf clover." Gloria was asking permission. Faye knew because she herself had carried that same tone with her own mother when that first time came.

Faye's spine tickled with that pride. She reached into her apron pocket and pulled out the gift for Gloria, who paused and stared. "Well, go on. Open it before we have an audience. You might need it sooner than you realize."

Gloria took a deep breath and pulled the tape off the end of the box, carefully unwrapping until wood showed through. She handed the wrapping to Faye and opened the oak box to reveal the smallest pair of gold-plated sewing scissors. The same gift her mother, Gloria's Great Grandmother—had gifted to Faye when Faye first married Albert.

Nestled next to the scissors was a tiny wooden bobbin of royal blue sewing thread and a minuscule bottle of super glue.

Gloria's blue eyes puddled with tears and her cheeks

flushed. She snapped the box shut and tucked it into her back jeans pocket. She threw her arms around Faye. "Thank you, Grandma."

"Melody's lucky to have a cousin like you." She kissed the girl's cheek. "What would the Crawley Crew do without us?"

Faye and Gloria joined their family for dinner. As the two ladies cleaned up the kitchen, Brian left in a huff, something about an allergic reaction to one of the sauces. Faye spotted Melody outside wrestling alone with the strands of the broken tree swing. She'd found a board in the garage and was attempting a repair.

Everyone else shook packages, sipped hot chocolate, or piled on the couch. Some stood and admired Faye's ever-growing collection of snowmen, recalling who gifted Faye which one. Which year, was it a Christmas gift five years past, or one of those summertime cabin things? The baby grand-daughter smiled slyly and nodded in understanding as Faye put a finger to her lips. No melting snowmen today. The secret would be kept.

The line of watch care over the Crawley Crew would continue. Faye could relax, knowing she'd passed the mantle into capable hands. Melody rejoined the group and hung close to Gloria's side after she'd fixed the swing.

And maybe, just maybe, there's the hope of more good help to come.

OF FAMILY AND FLANNEL

Sometimes history repeats itself despite our best efforts...

When it was time to choose a husband, I wanted a man who despised hunting, could hold an intelligent conversation, and never wore flannel. I found that man in Chris. I give him a peck on the cheek as he puts the glittering angel on top of the Christmas Tree. Evie will be home any minute with her fiancé, whom we've yet to meet or even see a photo of. Holidays are always hard on me, and this added drama—even though it promises to be positive drama—isn't helping anything.

I'm getting a son-in-law, sight unseen, whether I like it or not. Bad timing or not.

We hear a car door, then another. "Quick, Becky," Chris says—because heaven forbid our daughter and her fiancé should catch us actually living in our house. I shove and toss the hodgepodge of leftover décor into the large Rubbermaid tote and scoot the whole thing into the coat closet—careful not to knock loose the back panel where I've stowed my bits of my childhood.

Happy, muffled voices float up the drive and bounce off the front door. Chris opens it before Evie can burst in.

And there, next to my gorgeous blonde-haired daughter, stood a strong, tall young man.

In a flannel shirt.

FROM THE TIME I WAS FIVE, MY MOTHER TAUGHT ME TO make better choices in life than she had. Guiding, directing. Pointing out all the errors of her ways. Her lessons were subtle, running in the background of my life like a low hum of a far-off generator.

The Christmas Eve when I was ten years old, my father, who wanted all male offspring but was cursed with four daughters, thrust a rifle into my hands and declared me his "hunting buddy."

That's the only thing I got for Christmas that year. My sisters, all younger than me, each got a Barbie-knock-off doll. Two dolls were blonde, one was red-headed, just like my sisters. The only other red-headed person we'd ever seen was Uncle Gary.

I'd asked for ponytail holders and a novel. Any novel. I didn't care. They could dig a book out of the reject bin at the thrift store for all I cared.

But I got a gun one day early, not wrapped, because we had nothing for Mom to cook us on Christmas day— at least no protein, that is.

At ten years old, I had no interest in hunting nor being my father's buddy. I knew where the fried squirrel and venison stew on our family's rural table came from, and my sisters and I ate heartily on such occasions. I knew where the bacon in the butcher's case came from too—a real treat.

But that didn't mean I wanted to be a butcher.

Or the butcher's buddy.

I preferred homework and baking pies. I'd tuck my blonde curls into a bun on top of my head using one of the dingy rubber bands that came off the free weekly newspaper that I'd read word for word before Mom shredded it to bits for the worm beds.

Heck. I preferred tending the massive worm beds and compost piles in our back yard over spending any length of time with him.

But on that Christmas Eve, he told me to pull my hair out of my eyes because I needed to see what I was shooting at. By the look on my mother's face, the gift of the rifle had not been discussed with her.

Later, a sister would tell me Mom sobbed until she threw up.

My father was a giant, at least to a ten-year-old. He wore one of several long-sleeved flannel shirts. In the summer months, he'd take a couple of his oldest, most worn flannels and cut the sleeves off. He had shoulders that most daughters would've loved to have been hoisted up on to see the entire world. But my dad never gave any of us rides on his shoulders. Or his knees. But he was always in flannel.

He was a soft-spoken man, always a thousand miles away. He never raised his voice, and he never raised a hand to any of us. When he did speak, most of what he said didn't make sense to me. Paranoid from his years in the service and completely obsessed with conspiracy theories of all flavors, my father was always on the lookout for some unseen enemy.

Moving from the city and its cacophony of sounds and sirens to the smaller suburbs didn't help.

Moving from the burbs to the middle-of-nowhere to live off the land and off the grid didn't help.

The "prying eyes" changed from terrorists to aliens, from aliens to subterranean government spies, then back to terrorists. He wanted to pull us girls from the public school, but mom put her foot down. Hard. The school bus showing up at the end of our dirt drive for nine months out of the year was heaven. A break away from the odd life our parents created for us.

While we were at school, my father hunted.

While we were at home, my father hunted.

Night, day. Middle of the afternoon. Didn't matter. He and his flannel shirts and his guns. Always circling our fifty acres of woods on the lookout for the newest danger.

Sometimes he brought back food. Most of the time, despite the shots ringing out around the property, he came back empty-handed.

He'd always hunt alone, except for once a year around Thanksgiving dad's brother would come in from the city to try and shoot a turkey. Uncle Gary never managed to shoot a turkey, and the butcher had to come to his rescue every time. Uncle Gary had the money to buy a turkey. We did not.

But that year. That Thanksgiving, Uncle Gary never made it out to the boonies to go hunting with my father. Something about catching a cold and not wanting to bring it to us girls. "Maybe for Christmas."

But we never heard from him about Christmas.

So I became Dad's hunting buddy.

I remember the weight of the gun in my hands. I'd been around guns all my life, and the adults had been very clear that us girls weren't to touch them. We obeyed. We didn't like the noise they made, the blasts echoing through the forest and bouncing off the exterior walls of our little house and the shed out back. We knew that sound meant dinner, but we didn't have to like it.

I pulled my hair back with my last rubber band. We put on our heavy coats—mine was slightly too small and I wondered how I'd manage to simply walk through the snow in the forest, let alone maneuver the small rifle.

"Wayne, don't you think she needs practice first?" Mom's face was as pale as the flour she was working into a pie crust. "Can't it wait till tomorrow?"

"She's my kid. She'll be fine." He kissed Mom on the top of the head and nodded for me to go outside.

"That's what I'm worried about." Mom turned back to her pie, and we left out the front door.

As we trudged through the yard toward the tree line, my father told me the gun was loaded and to watch where I pointed it. That when the time was right, he'd show me how to aim and shoot. Then he didn't say much else unless I asked a question.

"Will I have to shoot a rabbit?" My stomach was churning in a thousand directions. I should've been freezing, but the nerves and the fear had me all numb.

"Maybe," Dad whispered, his eyes gazed at the tops of the trees. My eyes followed his.

"A squirrel?" I looked at his back—where his rifle should've been slung over his shoulder. It wasn't there. He hadn't brought his gun.

"Perhaps." He froze. His face as pale as Mother's in that instant.

"What's wrong?" I froze too.

He nudged me forward. "Something feels off. Something's not right."

At ten, I wasn't clued in to all of my father's mental issues, but I wasn't completely oblivious, either. "Something feels off. Something's not right" was his go-to phrase when he was about to leave the house and go hunting for hours on end, shooting bullets into the sky or the ground. Not bringing home food.

Then it happened...

His eyes darted further into the woods, well past where we were walking. Twigs snapped in the distance behind us. We spun around. He held up a hand. We stopped. I held my breath. I remember pleading and begging Mother nature not to send a deer across our path.

The red-brown movement against the snow-white and bleak gray forest caught my eye. Deer fur.

My father took my gun from me. I was happy to relinquish my sweaty grip on that tiny, but oh so heavy rifle. I watched as he readied the weapon, brought the sight up to his eye, and aimed at that red-brown movement.

A shot rung out, not from my firearm, but from somewhere else. A split second later, my father pushed me to the ground and then squeezed the trigger.

And again.

And again.

And then he fell on me, and all went black.

My next memory of that holiday was the following morning when I awoke to my sisters' squeals over their dolls and coloring books.

"Where's Dad?" I asked. Mom was in the kitchen, pouring Christmas morning cereal into our bowls. Four small bowls for us and one for her. "Where's Dad?"

Mom's eyes were red. Face still pale. "He's hunting. And this time he's not coming back."

I look to the corner by the front door. My new rifle was propped there. Mom had put a red bow around the barrel.

"Why isn't he coming back? I messed up, didn't I? Yesterday, I did something wrong—" I struggled to remember Christmas Eve's events. But when I closed my eyes, all I could remember was the cold and wet seeping through to my bones, and then seeing nothing but flannel, the zipper of Dad's jacket left undone, his brown and green flannel showing through...

"No. No, you did not." She grabbed my face in her hands and then buried my head into her chest and sobbed. "Dad went hunting. And Uncle Gary went with him and that's all you need to know. We won't speak of it anymore." Then, in a whisper, "Especially not to your sisters."

We stood there in the kitchen holding each other for a bit. Every time I blinked, I could see more clearly the flannel. The blood.

Hear the moans further into the distance.

Hear my father say one last time, as the weight of him pressed me into the cold ground, "Something feels off, Becky. Something's not right." And it wasn't right. It wasn't right at all.

A stunned tingle ran through my whole body and my knees didn't want to hold my frame upright. I hated that feeling. Of all the feelings I've ever felt, stunned is my least favorite. I've worked hard since to never feel that again.

"Check on your sisters. Shake it off, Beck." Mom returned to readying breakfast.

I went to the living room and picked up the scraps of plain brown Kraft paper Mom used to wrap the dolls. "I'll just take this mess out to the worms."

Mom dropped the gallon of milk to the table with a thud. "No. No, sweetheart." She grabbed the paper wads from my hands and kissed my blonde curls. "The worms have had enough."

MOM TAUGHT ME HOW TO MAKE PIES, A SKILL WHICH COMES in handy this time of year. Chris and I don't worry about putting food on the table. We've got turkey, ham, and all the trimmings waiting for their turn in the oven. I listen to the banter in the other room as I roll out the pie crust. I remember the wave of paleness that engulfed my mom's face the day I got the gun, white as flour.

I roll the pastry and listen as my soon-to-be-son-in-law spills out conspiracy theory after conspiracy theory. Chris makes polite "uh-huhs," and "I sees" as the kid rattles on. Evie chimes in, but I know my daughter — she's not buying any of his nonsense. But she's too naive and in love to stand her ground.

Mom taught me how to shake things off, bury things deep.

And she also taught me how to take care of matters on a permanent basis.

"Doin' okay, sweetheart?" Chris interrupts my thoughts and swipes a finger through the pie filling before planting a pumpkin spice-flavored kiss on my cheek.

Yeah. When it came time to choose a husband, I chose well. Mom would be proud.

"Just fine, Chris. I'll be there in a minute."

When it came time to choose a home, I went with a large two-story house with lots of windows placed firmly in suburbia. No forests to hunt or be hunted in. No long dirt lane for our children to catch the bus from. Concrete all around.

And though no fancy picket fence was necessary, a solid backyard privacy fence was a must, else what would the neighbors say?

Because aside from pie-baking and the ability to shake things off, I carried a complete and total obsession with composting and worm farms into my adulthood.

I wipe the flour on my apron, pour four large mugs of

spiced apple cider, and arrange them on a tray. I join my family in the living room.

"Thank you, Mrs. Avery," Evie's flannel-clad man said.

I force a smile and hand him a mug. "Call me Becky. We're going to be family someday, yes?"

He smiles, nods, and takes a sip of his cider. After a swallow and a big breath, he dives into tales of his last hunting trip with his uncle.

I settle onto the couch next to my daughter, kiss her on the cheek, and let my mug rest in my hands. I block out the Flannel Boy and Chris's polite replies. And my daughter's infatuation.

I close my eyes and think of the panel in the hall closet that hides my Christmas present from so many years ago — I even kept the red bow Mom had put on it.

"Ma'am?" Flannel Boy was saying.

I shake off my private stance. "Yes?"

He holds his mug toward me. "I'm sorry, but I'm not fan of cinnamon. Where should I put this?"

I stand and take his undrunk cider, and smile. "We have worms out back. They're always hungry for something different."

ALL THE BELLS AND
WHISTLES

Securing one's future never takes a holiday...

Marjorie arrived one hour early to Gary's Gavel Garage, or Three-G as the locals called it. She backed her pickup truck next to the old oak tree. Phil had done the driving and the backing up of the beast of a truck, and she was glad to have arrived early, allowing extra room to maneuver before the massive lot was tight with auction-goers all parked cattywampus. It took her three times in reverse to get the vehicle straight, using the tree's trunk and the lamppost as goalposts so as not to overshoot the lot and end up stuck in the muddy, harvested field.

She'd get better at it. Backing up. Driving.

Adjusting to life without him.

She prided herself on being a quick study. And she didn't mind practice.

The sky struggled to hold the last frail rays of the day, and in an hour, the temps would plummet, turning the late afternoon's drizzle into a glaze of ice over the nearly bare-of-gravel lot. The few loose rocks stubborn enough to not get swept away to the edges of the cornfields during the fall flooding would soon be imprisoned in frozen shackles.

She turned the engine off and stared at the old brick building. The light pole next to the tree buzzed to life, and the hum of the electricity running into the bulb penetrated through the moonroof's glass.

That hum.

Wow. How a memory rushes into one's brain from a simple sound.

Right here decades ago. Or, maybe, it was the security light opposite this one, but in this parking lot at any rate. But the hum was the same.

Thirty years ago with her first beau. He twenty, just starting pharmacy school, she eighteen and on the hunt for Mr. Right. And Triple G being the only entertainment for the locals for miles and miles...Well, half the county's offspring were likely conceived under the hum of these security lights.

Her twins certainly were.

She and Matt. Making out in his silver Dodge Viper. Under the hum of the light while a much younger Gary kept the gavel swinging, the crowd entertained, and the money flowing in.

She shook off the memory, rubbed her left side out of habit, and straightened the rearview mirror to check her face. She'd stopped the crying a week ago, so her eyes weren't puffy. They were bright tonight.

A few of the sobs had been truly hers and dealt lung-crushing blows. As they should've.

Most of the crying, though, was obligatory. For others—family, friends, undertakers—who believed she should still sob, given that this would be her first Christmas without her precious Phillip. Given that she'd already lost one husband.

Her twins, grown adults with kids of their own now, grieved the loss of their stepfather. And Matt. All new. All fresh tears.

Resurrected grief.

That caused her more pain than the actual loss did. Watching her children mourn. Jarod took it the hardest. He'd had more in common with Phillip than his own father. Woodworking. Auctions. Real estate.

Lots of time spent in the garage, those two.

But she'd stopped her tears. Brought the gavel down, so to speak.

Time to move on.

She reached into her pocket and pulled out a scrunchie. She wrestled her brown curls into a messy bun on top of her head. Brown from the drug store box, otherwise mouse-gray. Like some seventy-year-old. Too much grief and stress over the years pulled the pigment right out of the strands.

She straightened her glasses, glad those browns staring back at her remained full-colored. She touched up her makeup.

Phil had called this pre-auction ritual "puttin' on the war mask."

Ready to intimidate.

Ready to pounce.

Ready to hold her head and bidder card high when the time came.

She popped loose the seatbelt, slid from the driver's seat, and stretched out the spine kinks from the half-hour drive. She wasn't looking forward to the potentially slick drive home in the swimmy pickup, and she'd certainly not planned on returning to the auction house. Ever.

But Jarod, while cleaning out Phil's mess of tools and man toys, had inadvertently sent one of Marjorie's boxes to Gary's Gavel Garage to pad the grandchildren's college educations.

A box of vintage Christmas lights buried under back

issues of This Old House. That's why the mix-up. Marjorie had hidden this strand of lights under the magazines—Phil never read anything more than once—and tucked them away in the garage attic until she needed them again.

She'd needed them the week after Matt passed. The grandbabies were just small tots and Marj worried herself sick that those precious little bits would stumble onto her secret stash and get hurt. So the light strand became the solution.

She'd needed the strand again the week before Phil died, and she was ever so grateful she'd held onto the malfunctioning, fraying corded bulbs.

Cars and trucks poured into the lot as Marjorie pulled open the heavy metal door to the auction house. She made her way to the front row where she hung her coat on the back of a poorly padded chair, the yellow foam peeking through its maroon fabric.

"Always mark your spot," Phil would say.

The makeshift concession stand was just firing up. Gary's ancient Aunt Anne dutifully chilled water bottles and cans of generic soda in coolers of ice—even though the time of year and frigid temps would warrant brewing coffee, even the generic stuff, to warm the bones of the auction-goers. Marj ordered a diet lemon-lime and one hotdog fresh off the vintage roller—plain to avoid slopping, even though she'd have preferred relish and mustard. If she waited until she were truly hungry, the dogs would have rolled under the heat lamp to the point of shriveled leather.

Phil had liked them that way. Shriveled and dry.

Marjorie preferred hers juicer.

Aunt Anne handed Marj the dog nestled in a stiff white bun—likely leftover from last week's auction—and the soda can dripping with melting ice water. "I was just stricken when I heard of your loss. Stricken. But it's so good to see you back. He'll be missed. Food's on the house tonight. Refills, too." She slid Marj's well-worn bidder card across the glass countertop. Number 525 on a third-sheet of bright lime cardstock. Fraying at the edges. Aunt Anne was frugal, for sure.

Phil's pencil markings on the back brought a pang of remorse. But Marj shook it off. She knew, with time, those pangs and his pencil markings would fade away.

She and Phil had bid on and won many treasures over the years with number 525, and the lime green card was a replacement card. One had been yellow. One white. Marj tucked the card into her back jeans pocket and gathered her snack. "Thanks, Aunt Anne."

Marj remembered the lesson learned from when Matt passed. That people don't expect much from grieving widows, and charity abounds—at least in the early days after the funeral. She didn't insist on paying for the food, even though she was more than capable. Phil's death had left her more than set for years to come.

As had Matt's, frankly, successful pharmacist he'd become.

She and Jarod had argued over the speed at which he cleaned up Phil's belongings. The money wasn't an issue, she insisted. But she'd come to realize that's how Jarod grieved. Cleaning.

Purging.

Moving on.

But she couldn't move on completely without that one box...

Marj placed the unopened soda at her seat and went to the front of the retrofitted firehouse where two dozen long tables supported the night's shopping selections. Tonight was special for Triple G and would prove to be a crowd-pleaser.

Tonight, Gary had separated and saved up all things Christmas to auction off. Many here were hoping to see their antique and vintage holiday items go for hundreds of dollars —enough to pay for this year's expensive gift-giving. Others were here to spend. Seeking that special item for their yard or their tree.

Or something retro to drive them down Memory Lane with the top down.

The memory of Mark had just exited off Memory Lane outside under the hum of the lamp. He'd been fun. For a while. In real-time and in the memories. Even tattooed his name across her left rib. Right near her heart.

She reached up and felt his name through her sweater, dangerously close to remembering again. She withdrew her hand. Tonight, Marj needed to stay in her single-laned highway until the night was over.

She munched on her hot dog and, again glad to have arrived early, was able to finish before it got cold as she inspected the wares. Lights. Glass bulbs. Blow-up ornaments. Sleds hung from ropes from the ceiling—the kind with the wooden bases and metal skis.

Clothtique Santa figurines and Department 56 village pieces nearly buckled the tables' efforts to hold them up.

On the display directly in front of the podium, she spied the box of goodies that she was hoping would be there, hoping that Gary had found the lights under the old magazines and set them aside for tonight. She made note of the lot number and took her seat before locals and travelers-from-afar came pouring in shoulder-to-shoulder to catch glimpses of their hearts' holiday decor desires.

Three bay doors large enough for bucket trucks and fire engines lined one wall, letting in the humidity in the summer and the frigid chill in the winter. Gary'd never bothered to replace the doors with true walls. Said it was easier to unload in the auction items often brought by truckfuls from estates of the dead and homes of those elderly downsizing for assisted living.

Just last year, Gary had installed an industrial heater above the doors. That side of the audience cooked under the glowing, humming element, while bidders across the aisle clung to their coats. The regulars—the looky-loos who lived in the one-stop-sign town with nothing better to do than attend Gary's auction every Friday night—took turns swapping sides of the aisle. Drove Gary nuts, as he'd get in a rhythm with the bidders, then they'd switch up seats. But the teamwork helped stave off the cold and kept butts in the seats until the auction ended.

An older couple, older than Marj by at least ten years, started arguing at one of the tables. The man wanted the plastic mold Santa with the huge crack in his hat. She said no. He said "but the grandkids" and she said "grandkids are into iPods, not old Santas." On and on they went.

She popped open her soda and took a sip, and slid it under her chair. Another couple—much younger, just starting out—argued over the top dollar they'd part with to bid on a vintage outdoor nativity scene. She wanted to go all out. He didn't, seeing as how the infant Christ was cracked and all. And, by the young man's account, one camel and a shepherd were MIA.

She entertained herself with others' conversations as she waited for starting time. She and Phil had given a garage-full of items to be auctioned off over the years—many of the same items the couple had won at Triple G were auctioned again, the money recouped, and bid out again on new finds the following Friday night.

Phil had been fun. For a while.

And not to be outdone by a love long lost, Phil insisted she tattoo his name on the rib just beneath Matt's. "It's part of your journey. How you've become the amazing woman you are. I think it's a beautiful thing." Phil was a good sport.

She resisted the urge to touch her ribs again and readjusted in her seat, stretching out her legs in front of her, careful not to kick anyone or to knock over her soda. Phil had unknowingly spilled his once, and the sugary cola—it had been summertime—seeped across the slightly slanted floor, soaking into a neighboring bidder's win tucked under her chair—a leather baseball glove. By the time the night was over, some dutiful ant scout had called for reinforcements and a whole army of soldiers had slid under the poorly insulated bay door and into the woman's glove.

What a ruckus that'd been. What fun. For a while.

She leaned back in her seat and checked her watch. Almost starting time. The buzz in the building drowned out the buzz from the overhead heaters. When Marj had realized the box with the light strand was missing, she'd panicked. Then she'd called the auction house after Jarod had dropped the load of Phil's stuff. Gary'd told her everything was buried under several loads of wares. "Lots of deaths this time of year. Lots of deaths. So sorry. But if it's Christmas, Bells and Whistles Night would be your best bet."

Bells and Whistles. Gary's catch phrase turned massive Christmas-auction-event.

All the bells and whistles.

Gary offered to let her come early this morning. Look through the setup. Give her the box back. But Marj hadn't wanted special treatment.

She never did after a death. She told herself it was because she was such a strong woman.

But likely she feared that her guilt would show through the grief. So she tried to keep her head down.

Marjorie also truly enjoyed the adrenaline rush of the bidding. That rush (Phil had described it as well, and Matt had a similar sensation when the kids were born and they'd started playing T-ball) probably kept Phil on this side of the ground longer than what Marj had originally planned.

He could be fun sometimes, after all.

And this item, this particular strand of lights? Well. Ben Franklin himself would be so proud that Marj had reversed engineered the 1950's bulbs. That day after Matt died. When the grandtots were toddling in her bathroom after the funeral, dangerously close to Marj's recipe. Dangerously close to their grandfather's cause of death.

And she couldn't let harm come to those tots.

Not ever. Not the kids. That's where she drew the line.

But she also drew the line at disposing of the amber glass bottle with Matt's MedShoppe label and its precious contents. One never knew when the need to be free—or simply unburdened from boredom—would burn a hole in her soul...

Well. That was also the day she'd dropped the box and one of the bulbs broke, spilling the liquid into the cardboard box and soaking through and the idea came to her. She'd strip the glass candle bits from their red and green heater bases. And replace the liquid inside with her recipe.

And into the attic they'd go, and no one would be the wiser.

And the little ones would be safe.

For good measure she ripped out portions of the wires in the cord, mimicking mouse activity as closely as possible, so no one would plug the set in. She believed herself wickedly intelligent, but she didn't have enough recipe left to experiment with. To see what would happen if an electric current shot through the lights filled with her own concoction.

Ah, the adrenaline. She wiped her hands, now sweaty with excitement, onto her jeans and reached for her soda.

Tonight would likely be the last true adrenaline rush she'd be afforded for quite some time.

Now that Phil was gone.

Because he'd stopped being fun.

And tonight, for All the Bells and Whistles, Aunt Anne

would even break out the popcorn machine. Though, she'd likely burn the first few batches as her old brain struggled to member how the popper worked.

Over the years, Phil and Marjorie had learned never to attend Triple G on those nights when their own belongings were auctioned off. Marj never cared what price her stuff brought. It was just stuff, after all.

But Phil had an unruly attachment to anything he'd ever spent a dime on and would bark and complain that his prized electric drill hadn't brought over five dollars—even though the cord was mouse-chewed and it had no bits. He'd complained that their old dining room furniture should've brought a fortune—vintage, it was—even though the box-store set had deep scratches and wobbly legs. And the Christmas tree? How dare the audience at Gary's not understand the value of his artificial baby? Didn't they know that new trees cost over fifty bucks? His should've brought at least half that, but it only went for a dollar—and to one of the cheapest, dirtiest bidders in the room.

How dare Gary not work harder to engage his crowd and run up the bids? How dare those Vanna Whites (the helpers —men and women both—parading the object up for bid all over the auction floor for the audience to admire) not work the crowd?

That did it for Marj, and she'd told Phil she'd never attend another auction when their things were up for bid.

Tonight she was breaking her own rule. But just for the one box.

She pulled her bidder card and sat it on her lap. Twinges of fear prickled her neck when someone would pick up the box with the special strand in it. That fear intensified to electric shocks when yet another auction-goer extended the strand out of the box, allowing the bulbs to dangle from their hands to the ground.

And inspected the cord.

The frayed cord. Don't plug it in. It won't work.

She could just see the current zipping through the old wires, exploding the liquid, her special formula, all over the firehouse's concrete.

And she couldn't make any more.

With Matt's death, she had no more access to the ingredients. How carefully she'd planned each visit all those years ago to his drugstore. Bringing him lunch during the hour the shoppe was closed to customers. Or picnic baskets of fried chicken and apple pie on the evenings he'd have to do inventory and quarterly insurance reports. Carefully slipping in three capsules of one drug. Five tablets of another. Slowly, so the pharmacy techs wouldn't notice the shortages.

One visit at a time.

One ingredient at a time.

Despite the urge to jump and grab the strand and go running from the building into the cold night, she stayed in the poorly padded maroon seat.

And enjoyed the surge of adrenaline.

She remained in her seat and tightened her bun. Game face, Marj. Game face.

Then she saw Dale. She'd missed seeing him enter as her focus was on the last woman to inspect her strand.

Dale.

Matt's brother. Slightly younger. Always more handsome. Far more successful than Matt or Phil.

But always just out of reach.

And had he aged well. Where Matt and Phil had simple frames and features, Dale was all muscle. A man's man. No gut. Guns heaving through the sleeves of his white button-up as he hoisted a wrought iron snowman doorstop above his head to inspect the bottom.

Classy. A peppering of gray in his black curls. Dignified even in jeans and loafers.

He replaced the doorstop and turned toward another table. Facing Marj.

He caught sight of her. Staring.

Her face blushed despite her best effort to keep the blood flow more south. He smiled.

She smiled.

He came toward her and asked if anyone was sitting next to her. He smelled nice. His heady cologne overtook the burning popcorn aroma.

"I'm so, so sorry Marj. I should've stayed in touch, but..." He hung his head.

"It's alright, Dale. It was a little too awkward, even for me. Even for the twins." Dale had moved to be closer to his parents five states away long before Matt died. The brothers hadn't been very close, and Marj's kids barely knew this man. Mostly they knew of him. "How've you been?" She dared not make eye contact. Not yet.

Game face, Marj. Game face.

He hung his head again and rubbed his left side. A motion Marj was familiar with, though she doubted Dale had a list of lovers tattooed under his heart. "Gracie passed a few months back. I'm here settling some estate issues from way back. Heard about the auction. Thought it'd be a nice distraction. Nostalgic, maybe, for old-time's sake."

"I understand." She fought hard to control her voice. The adrenaline was about to bubble right out of her ears. The auction. The bubble lights. Dale. Newly widowed. The impending weather. The bad drive home. Dale.

Gary took his place on the podium and Dale asked if he could sit with Marj.

"Of course."

The microphone popped to life. The crowd hushed.

"Welcome folks on this nasty cold night. We've got all the bells and whistles tonight, and here's the rules..." Gary went on and on and then he started.

Santas rolled out the door.

Then snowmen. Dale bid on and won the doorstop. A congratulatory fist bump.

Angels flying off the tabletops right and left.

The old nativity set went for pennies, and the young couple won. Happy even with a cracked Jesus and missing livestock.

Sleds were lowered from the ceiling and carted to vehicles outside.

Then the table of vintage lights. Marj bid on and won a random box, so as not to seem overeager when her special strand came up. Gary bid on a box and won, as well.

Her box was called up. The helper in the front of the room pranced the strand back and forth for all to see. The beautiful 1950s bubble lights, only needs a new cord. Not hard. On and on Gary went, trying to seduce more bidder cards into the air. She readied number 525.

Dale readied his card. 986.

Surely not. Marj tried to remain focused.

Dale bid first. Marj jumped. Then remembered to slip her card in the air.

Dale grinned at her. He knows.

His card went up. Then her card. He can't know.

Every pore seeped. She was sure she'd reek by the time this was over.

His 986 again. Gary had reached a singsong rhythm with the calling, swaying back and forth. "Ten, now fifteen, now twenty..."

Marj stood, knocking over her lemon-lime onto Dale's leather loafers. "One hundred dollars." The crowd gasped and some clapped.

Gary, most likely out of charity, yelled "Sold!" and slammed his gavel down with flare before Dale could react to anything but the dampening of his feet. Good ol' Gary. She smiled at him and went to retrieve her box from the hands of the old man Vanna White.

She returned to her seat and retrieved her coat.

"Leaving? Now? After that? You're just getting started," Dale said, still flicking drops from his feet.

"I...I'm sorry about your shoes. I just really like these lights." She tried to be coy.

"I'd say." He stood as the auction buzzed on around them. "Walk you out? It's dark and slick."

She accepted his gesture and the pair exited the side of the building into the parking lot. As Marj had feared, the dark and dipping temps had indeed frozen the parking lot over. Dale took the box from her and slid a strong arm under hers. "You'll make it home alright?"

"Yeah." She wasn't sure. "They've likely treated the roads."

"Likely. But in case. You have a cell, right?"

She nodded. They reached the truck. She slid behind the wheel. He opened the passenger door and placed the box carefully on the seat next to her. "Give me your number. Call me if you get stuck. Or..."

Marj took a chance. Straightened her back. Held head a little higher, as high as her bidder card. "Where will you be for Christmas?"

He shuffled then shrugged. Smiled.

She smiled.

"Come to the house. We'd be happy to have you." She fished her cell from her back pocket and they exchanged numbers.

"I'll think about it. I'll think about it."

She started the engine and let it warm while Dale walked back to brick firehouse. Triple G. What a night. She pulled straight forward, careful to allow the truck tires time to grip the frozen lot. She had to be careful. She swung out to the road. Still slush. Not ice. Not yet.

She relaxed a little as the headlights led the way. She rested her right hand in the box of bubble lights. Her fingers played with the cord. With the green and red bases. With the glass tips housing the secret formula.

And she smiled. Having Dale for Christmas would be fun.

For a while.

Marj had few more lights.

She had few more ribs.

She had all the bells and whistles for her next happily ever after.

THE PRISTINE PAPER CHAIN

What's real? What's not? What does it matter when you're a rock star?

I tuck the last of three plastic bins into the trunk of my rusted blue Civic. Bins that carry my yearly offering to the great and mighty staff at Rockport Palms. I cram my beat-up carry-on next to the totes so nothing will shift on the ten-minute drive across town. Last year the totes slid on the carpet, popping the lids off and spilling the contents before I reached my destination. I double-check the cargo. I don't want to arrive in shambles this year. I don't want my offering marred or bent, either.

Satisfied with my packing job, I slam the lid shut and stretch my back out. The thud turns the head of the next-door neighbor out to gather his newspaper from his stoop. I nod a polite greeting. Henry nods back slowly and smiles, then hangs his head, unsure of what to say or do next. He'd have likely lingered on the stoop, soaking up the morning rays despite the chill in the air. We had a deep snow the last week of November, but that's nearly gone, and everyone is emerging from their icy Thanksgiving cocoons, eager to enjoy a few 40-degree days before December reaches up with its bony fist and punches us all down again, Midwestern style.

Henry knows I'm about to disappear for a chunk of days. Soon the whole street will know. Not because Henry will tell them, but because it's my pattern to disappear. Henry and his wife to my right, Annabelle and her ever-growing brood of children to my left, and someone down the road will surely inform the new-to-the-cul-de-sac newlyweds across the street that Megan Lynch will be off the grid until the first of the year. A peaceful holiday season for all.

I walk around the Civic, kicking the tires. Checking the patches of rust, twice as big as this time last year. In a year or two, if I don't total the car, the rust will have eaten through the back floorboards—there's already a spot on the front passenger side carpeting that gets wet when I drive through puddles. Where the road salt and lack of upkeep on my part chewed through the flooring.

But the trunk is dry, though, and that's the most important. It's only a ten-minute drive to Rockport Palms, and my offering this year includes reams of red and green construction paper, rolls of transparent tape (I bought out the local dollar store's stock), a dozen bottles of white school glue, a dozen safety scissors picked up once the school supplies hit the shelves, and two gallons of glue to refill the smaller bottles. It's my biggest and best offering yet. I always feel somehow more welcome when I show up with a trunk full like this.

Soon, I'll join the mighty ranks at the crafting table, chanting "Dot, dot, not a lot," and "Dab, dab, just a dab," as I help the aged ones squeeze glue onto strips of red and green to create their holiday paper chains. I'll add more than a few of my own links, too, allowing the monotonous task to wash away the holiday stress and chaos raging outside Rockport Palms' walls. I'll ignore the fact that my hands are nowhere near as wrinkled as theirs. My skin is not dotted with liver spots or sectioned off with bulging webs of veins. My joints are not riddled with arthritic knots.

I don't fit in at Rockport.

But I absolutely belong at Rockport.

High-pitched squeals erupt from one or more of Annabelle's children, bringing me back to the present. Their tiny hands try to snowball-up the remaining muddy slush. They wave at me, mittens dripping. I wave back. They'd have a lot of fun with the stuff in my trunk. But it's not for them. It's for my comrades at Rockport.

It feels normal. This street. The families tucked away in the cookie-cutter two-story homes. Christmas decorations popping up on lawns (or laying in deflated messes, as the case may be), tendrils of smoke coming from chimneys here and there. Plastic candy cane ornaments lining the paved drives all the way to the doors.

Mine is the only home with no Christmas cheer spilling into the yard. There's no holiday cheer inside, either. I won't be home for Christmas. I can only hope Dave won't be home, either.

I glance up to my own second-story window. Dave walks past, the lace curtain of my bedroom signaling his movement. He appears again briefly in the spare bedroom's window. He's pristine. He does it on purpose. Perfect hair. Perfect clothing. Teeth white as snow.

Always pristine.

I stretch one last time and get in my car. Annabelle hangs out her front door, yelling at her kids. She sees me. The same look of realization races across her face as had Henry's just moments ago. She waves. A polite smile. I return the wave as I back out of my drive.

I stifle the urge to wave goodbye to Dave.

I'm blessed they tolerate me, my neighbors, given what Dave and I put them all through a few years back. After my meltdown hit the newspapers and those newspapers hit the stoops of every cul-de-sac in the 'burb, Dave stopped being my rock.

Dave never was my rock, because Dave never even, well...

Where our cul-de-sac meets the main road, I pause at the stop sign. This is part of my ritual on my way to Rockport, as much so as the offering in my trunk is. Time freezes for me here. The neighbors know to go around me. It's not a busy road. They give me my space.

It's actually the worst part of the drive. This stop sign. On my own road. Turn signal ticking off the seconds as the remaining frost burns off the windshield. I crack the window to breathe fresh air as I remember in technicolor detail how this season came to be for me...

Dave Hanson. My childhood sweetheart. I clung to him like glue after my family passed in the car crash. He was my ever-present friend. There for me all through my college years, cheering me through masters and doctorate work. All through my CEO years.

We finally married. A pristine, private ceremony in Panama City Beach. I kept my maiden name. Dave didn't mind, due to my success in the business world. Dave was the one that encouraged me to take the job in Indianapolis— bigger fish and smaller pond than NYC. Live in the quaint country suburb. Commute to the city. Win the awards. Take the Fortune 500 company to new heights. Garner national attention in all the right niches.

"Megan Lynch, you're gonna be a rock-star," Dave would tell me.

Until the market died and my dream died with me and Dave Hanson turned nag extreme. "You gotta keep the attention on you. Show 'em who's the best CEO in the nation, Meg. Never forget you're a rock star. My rock star." At Dave's insistence, I arrived at the Thanksgiving office party wearing my lavender bikini, modified with brown and yellow tail feathers from the dollar store crafting aisle, strutting all my stuff, and got fired on the spot. But not before a half dozen cell phones captured the debacle.

I wrapped myself up in my overcoat and drove back to my grand two-story cookie-cutter house where I took a golf club from Dave's collection and dared him to come outside and face me.

He did. I swung.

He yelled. I swung and yelled.

As hard as I swung, I could never make contact. Dave was nowhere and everywhere, and I couldn't track him in my rage. My overcoat unbuttoned with all the swinging, revealing skin and flashes of lavender.

Henry and Annabelle and their respective families came to my aid. Yelling my name. Yelling for 911. For a split second I wondered why no one was yelling at Dave...

I shiver back to the present, the blinker in my Civic continues to count down the seconds. The heater has taken care of the frost, but the breeze through my open window is too cold now.

I gently turn right out of my tiny neighborhood. I know the trunk is packed tightly, but I take it easy, anyway. A mile past my road and the clumps of houses turn into sprawling farmland. Remnants of tan corn stalks poke through the melting snow. The pavement turns from smooth to rough and chunked out from farm equipment wear. In a county slowly losing population and funds to fix the roads.

Rockport Palms is a few miles ahead.

The first time I visited Rockport, it was under a 72-hour hold issued by a nameless, faceless judge who'd likely signed dozens of such orders that week. The holiday season six years ago was rife with all manner of stressed-out folks who couldn't cope one way or another. The facilities that catered to people like me, successful, active and alive businesspersons were full up. The only two beds open in the state. One was for juveniles, and they don't tend to throw adults in with the kids. The other was at Rockport, a geriatric mental health holding spot where my breakdown didn't fit in with the Alzheimer's flare-ups, senile dementia issues, and general end-of-life decline. My age didn't either. I was a spry thirty-four-year-old woman. These patients were in their seventies and up. Some were more like four-year-olds mentally.

My first forty-eight hours at Rockport were spent ranting, raging and raving about how I didn't belong. Throwing up the medication cocktail. Throwing tissue boxes. Throwing fits.

Swearing Dave would show up in his pristine-ness and sign me out and take me home.

And all the while knowing he wouldn't.

Then I met Gretta Bristow. Who spoke to her dead husband four times a day and swore he was coming to sign her out and take her home. We'd sit and make paper chains. I was later told this craft was an exercise in fine motor skills to aid in the physical therapy portion of treatment. I told them with two middle fingers that my fine motor skills were right as rain, but the staff ignored me.

We placed our initials on each strip before taping or gluing the paper ends together, hooking one inside the next, inside the next. Me and Gretta initialing and gluing and taping. GB. ML. GB. ML. Young, smooth hands and old, spotted ones. Hours at the crafting table. When we were busy chaining, we weren't ranting, and the staff just let us be until it was time for therapy.

Gretta didn't know she was even in therapy.

But I did. So they focused on me. And they focused on Dave.

They'd remind me over and over: Megan Lynch, you're an accomplished businesswoman. No children, no pets, and as it turns out, no husband. No Dave Hanson.

Though I debated them on that last point multiple times during my first admission. That was the weekend after Thanksgiving.

I debated it again on my second seventy-two-hour hold ordered by the same nameless, faceless judge the weekend before Christmas of the same year. When Dave popped his head in the kitchen and asked if dinner was ready yet. It was ready. Meatloaf and mashed potatoes and salad, table set for two, but that wasn't the point.

We got into another "domestic disturbance" that spilled into the front lawn in shin-deep snow, me in my threadbare pajamas, and Dave, as always, pristinely dressed in designer jeans and a turtleneck yelling at me to be a rock star. I demanded to know why he left me in that hellhole Rockport with rotting old bodies, and Henry and Annabelle once again demanded to know who I was talking to, this time swinging a butcher knife in lieu of a golf club.

Gretta was there for that admission too. I don't know if she was readmitted or if she'd stayed the course while I was on furlough to my own home. We resumed our paper chain. The staff helped us hang it down the hall. By the time I was discharged, the chain stretched four times the length of the main hallway, up and down. Mostly the greens and reds were mine and Gretta's...

She won't be here this year. She passed away after my third trip to Rockport. At least she can speak to her husband face-to-face now.

Mine is a figment of my imagination. Or so they tell me.

Over the last few years, ten years to be exact, the paper chains grew and I had to fight to keep those first ones in the loop, so to speak. Mine and Gretta's. Now so aged, the reds have turned to pinks and the greens to a winter-dreary gray. That's part of my ritual, too. Finding those links in the chain, spotting our initials. Remembering the names of the others that added to the handmade garland.

The Civic rolls into the parking lot of Rockport Palms. The signage at the corner of the lot sported palm trees around the facility's name. Palms. What an asinine name. Middle of Indiana. Middle of farmville. Palms? The company founders started this chain in Florida and didn't bother with a name change for the midwestern branches. I turn the car off and pop the trunk.

I'm pleased to see that my packing this year was much better than last. I remove the totes and carry them one at a time to the front glass entry doors. Once I have my suitcase, I ring the buzzer. I hope my offering will be accepted. Reams of paper. Gallons of glue. New scissors. Never has one of my offerings been rejected. Perhaps it's my jolly holiday spirit.

Or perhaps it's the hefty out-of-pocket down payment I lay out each spring to hold my bed for the impending holiday months. When Dave shows up. And I need paper chain therapy.

A blue-scrubbed mental health technician comes to the door. She's new. These employees always are. The therapist and docs stay the same, though. The turnover for mental health techs is high. The fists to the face, the dirty adult diapers, the food dribbling out of the mouths of the overly medicated.

It's a glamourless job.

I try not to add to their burden. At least not anymore. Or at least not yet, not until I'm Gretta's age and medicated beyond belief. I've got a couple of decades to go before then.

The tech looks confused. Patients don't show up with totes of crafting supplies. Most come in ambulances or accompanied by distraught and overwhelmed loved ones.

Neil appears. Neil is the therapist that reminds me Dave isn't real three times a week on weekdays. He says something to the tech, whose eyes widen in understanding. They both nod and unlock the door.

My reputation precedes me.

"Woah, Megan. What a load!"

I feel the tension in my shoulders release and I exhale. They've accepted my offering with glee. I allow them to carry the totes while I wheel in my suitcase. I glance behind me toward the Civic. I won't see her or drive her until the New Year as Rockport Palms swallows me into the geriatric therapeutic wing.

Neil, not waiting for proper intake paperwork or the therapy room shoots a glance at me. "So, Megan. Dave been bothering you or did we catch the admission just in time?"

I remember Dave moving around in the house before I left. "I haven't seen him this year. I think we're catching it in time." I lie because I want to get to the crafting table and meet my new gang of paper chain makers with a non-medicated head.

Get them started on the cutting and the pattern of red, green, red, green.

Dot, dot, not a lot.

Dab, dab, just a dab.

I'll come clean in a few days. I definitely don't want Dave waiting for me come January.

"Your old paper chain is ready. Dug it out of storage this morning. It's getting flatter by the year. May be hard to hang. Needs some repair, kind of brittle..."

"Thanks, Neil. That's okay. I'm looking forward to the trip down memory lane. With Gretta and all."

I spend the next half hour with the tech who pushes paperwork and searches me and my belongings for smuggled drugs or sharp objects. I give her my tennis shoes and don my new memory foam slippers.

I turn my phone over. I work from home now, and my virtual clients have been told I'm taking leave. They're used to the routine. I work like a dog the first ten months out of the year so I can spend the last two in Rockport.

Neil takes charge of the scissors (only the most capable and docile of patients can use them under supervision) and leads me to my room, a shared space with an octogenarian named Ola Mae. Ola Mae sleeps most of the day, he tells me, but I bet if she's here long enough, I can recruit her into my chain gang.

We go straight to the craft room—therapy doesn't start until after lunch. The walls are littered with stick-figure and scribble drawings as if kindergarteners raided the cabinets. Neil nods to a corner where my very first paper chain waits for my inspection and repairs. I pull the chain from its box, the pale pink reds and the drab grey greens greet me. Many have Gretta's initials. GB. The rest are mine, ML, until the paper turns brighter and more patients' initials add to the garland.

I dig out the tape from my tote and shore up a few spots, getting the garland ready for Neil and a staff member to begin hanging the chain up and down the halls of Rockport.

Then something catches my eye as I pull the very end out of the box. From the Gretta Days. From that first admission. A bright red chain link where there should've been only pale, faded ones. Ones with only GB and ML: Gretta Bristow and Megan Lynch.

This one had different initials.

Initials that I'd never seen before at Rockport Palms.

I wipe my palms, now drenched in sweat on my sweatpants. I close my eyes and chant under my breath over and over. "Megan Lynch. You are a single woman. No children. No pets. And no husband."

I look down at the crisp red loop in our paper chain.

DH.

"There is no Dave Hanson."

I fish through the rest of the chain, stopping again and again at pristine, crisp red loops where there should not have been crisp anything. DH. DH. DH.

"You have no husband."

I fish around for the beginning of the chain and inspect closer that very first bright red out-of-place link. I lost my breath.

Just before the bold DH. In tiny, pristine block letters.

Get well soon, rock star.

ABOUT THE AUTHOR

Beth enjoys chucking words into sentences then standing back to see what magic—or mayhem—falls out, crafting tales in mystery, sci-fi, fantasy, and general "slice of life" fiction. She couldn't accomplish this without the help of her tutu-clad Little Miss Muse and Trudi the Concrete Office Goose, who's partial to superhero capes.

Her stories have appeared in multiple publications, including Pulphouse Fiction Magazine and Ellery Queen Mystery Magazine, and in multiple fiction anthologies. She's received several Honorable Mentions from Writers of the Future. Her lighthearted blog peeks into the writing life as she pokes fun at herself and her circus of a life.

Follow the antics of Little Miss Muse and Trudi, read Beth's blog (she might have burned down her kitchen last week), and discover the stories at bapaul.com.

Short Story Collections

Spunk and Spice, Volumes 1 and 2: A Collection of six short stories celebrating timeless wit and wisdom.

Out There, Volumes 1 and 2: A Collection of six short sci-fi and speculative tales.

Mystery Minutes, Volumes 1 and 2: Six short mystery stories

All the Feels, Volumes 1, 2, and 3: Collections of inspiring short stories

Just a Tick of Whimsy, Volumes 1 and 2: Collections of fantasy shorts.

Dark Minds: Toe-curling twisted mysteries.

Blog Compilations: Slices of the writing life with lots of laughs and bumps in the road.

Life Along the Way

Life All Over Again

Novels

Triage

Young Adult (or Young at Heart) Books

Switch: Book 1 in the Oliver Andrews Trilogy

STAY IN TOUCH!

BAPAUL.COM

Take a glimpse into B.A. Paul's writing journey, including the ups and downs of managing family, "real jobs," ducks in wobbling rows, and chasing down her Little Miss Muse. New blog posts go up Mondays, with the first Monday of the Month reserved for a free fiction short story available on the blog for a limited time.

Newsletter Signup!

Get the latest release information, author updates, and exclusive content by signing up with your email. Check out bapaul.com.

9 781964 800059